This novella is a great single or multiple session read. The book is incredibly well researched, with an accurate depiction of life on the river and the journey down the waterways. Roberts knows his boats, the Tonle Sap, and his weapons, moreover, he fits seamlessly into the Cambodian 'fishing lifestyle.'

After many years as an expatriate, Roberts' bests friends are Cambodian people, and many see him as a brother. In a positive way, with intellect, and a chess board, he assists in the lives of his friends and those whom he calls his family. He is honest, with a touch of a romantic soul, and more than a touch of cheeky larceny.

The oriental setting is both beautiful and yet menacing. The characters, in this book, are sharp, true to life, and the action, dynamic. Who could not like, "MR ROBERTS ON THE TONLE SAP AND MEKONG."

Roberts is a true 'Australian Hero' in a world of uncompromising superpowered nations hell bent on ruling Indochina.

– Carlos Geagea
B.A. English and Dramatic Art, Dip.Ed.

Dr Vish Khan was born to humble beginnings, but soon, at the young age of 23 years, his genius in Mathematics, Physics and Engineering was recognized with multiple degrees and a doctorate in Theoretical Physics. He was married at 24 years of age to an Australian girl of Italian descent. He has two adult sons.

To my wife, Rosa, who puts up with my madness and loves me as much as I love her. To my sons, Christopher and Matthew, who I trained to be hopefully kinder and better men than me.

A novella, written for fun, in February and March 2023.

I hope you enjoy the story.

Dr Vishwamitra Khan

Mr Roberts On The Tonle Sap And Mekong

Austin Macauley Publishers™
LONDON · CAMBRIDGE · NEW YORK · SHARJAH

Copyright © Dr Vishwamitra Khan 2024

The right of Dr Vishwamitra Khan to be identified as author of this work has been asserted by the author in accordance with sections 77 and 78 of the Copyright, Designs and Patents Act 1988.

All rights reserved. No part of this publication may be reproduced, stored in a retrieval system, or transmitted in any form or by any means, electronic, mechanical, photocopying, recording, or otherwise, without the prior permission of the publishers.

Any person who commits any unauthorised act in relation to this publication may be liable to criminal prosecution and civil claims for damages.

This is a work of fiction. Names, characters, businesses, places, events, locales, and incidents are either the products of the author's imagination or used in a fictitious manner. Any resemblance to actual persons, living or dead, or actual events is purely coincidental.

A CIP catalogue record for this title is available from the British Library.

ISBN 9781035839698 (Paperback)
ISBN 9781035839704 (ePub-e-book)

www.austinmacauley.com

First Published 2024
Austin Macauley Publishers Ltd®
1 Canada Square
Canary Wharf
London
E14 5AA

Thank you also to Austin Macauley and their staff for their assistance with my first Novella.

Dr Vishwamitra Khan instructs that this is a work of FICTION, and the story is entirely his. No individual mentioned exists in real life, and Dr Vish hopes and prays that nations around the world, will stop playing GAMES and act more responsibly towards the lives of people of Indochinese nationality. Dr Vish thanks the Cambodian people for their generous support and affection. They are the most generous, and loving society in the world.

In recent times, they have endured a holocaust, a civil war, and the hopeless regret of being almost unaided in this changing world. What has been referred to by the British as *'The Great Game'*, was played out in recent times, with Cambodia as a pawn. The result of that game is well known to all thinking humans. The reality is that we, first-world nations, owe a debt to Cambodia for the way that they have endured without becoming a bitter and twisted society, such as a few others, that I will not mention here.

There should be, no empire-building and no political games in Indochina. At what stage of its development does a powerful nation stop trying to control other nations? Let's amuse ourselves by saying, now. And with a little luck and a little fortitude, maybe we just might keep out of the affairs of other nations. As my mother used to say, "It's all fun and games until someone loses an eye."

Chapter 1
A Killing Affair

So many foreign countries, and so much intrigue, in the "Big Game", but this has unfortunately never changed, in the sovereign nation of Cambodia. Wars come and wars go, but in the region of Indochina and even in peacetime, superpowers continue the search for changes in the political and social structure of nations, indeed, to change those structures to their own benefit, to bend nations to their collective and differing wills, if they can.

Several figures of men moved through the darkened streets of Siem Reap. All entered an ally way, approaching one another, from opposite directions. The ally was small and rather cramped, in all, no more than a hundred metres in length, varying in width from two to three metres, pungent smells emanating from the cobbled dark ground, and grey putrid walls. Garbage amassed on both sides of this dark path, with only rats, some as large as cats to call this place home. Each of the men moved with desperate purpose, and knowledgeable precision, pistols, and automatic weapons at the ready.

With hand gestures alone, a taller man, gave the order for his two comrades to spread to opposite sides of the small laneway, just a pathway between slightly larger streets, while he maintained the middle ground—the most dangerous place to be—and with a commander's determination, only slightly ahead of his men. Behind these men an expensively dressed woman trailed, covered with a cloak, her 9 mm Glock in hand, and like the others, she was prepared for war.

The approaching force of four did similarly, only the men travelled two by two, each gaining the slightest cover from garbage and the surrounding walls. And those trailing behind, some extra cover from the men in front. The leader of this group carried a very full, medium-sized duffle bag. Its size and weight made his movements appear a little strained but not particularly awkward. These men were all young, strong men, the pride of their nation and trained to the highest standard.

The parties converged, and with what appeared to be a friendly word between the leaders; the duffle bag was offered and the tall man accepted it with a degree of thanks, and once the straps were taken, even before releasing the opposite person's hand, he fired only one shot through the head of the other. The man was dead, long before he or his pistol hit the pavement. His life flowed into the infinite ether and with it the fragile peace that existed between the groups. The two men on either side of their tall boss, without hesitation, opened fire killing their opponent, sending the final two, now outnumbered but not outgunned into defensive fire from small calibre fully automatic weapons. The "cracks" splintering the peace of the night and the sleep of residents. The tall man and his men appeared to have won the day, rushing forward, and shooting the last two opponents in the head as they tried to flee a worsening situation. The tall man's crew had won the fire fight and for the briefest of moments, a level of quiet returned with only a few residents protesting the untimely noise and fireworks.

The woman, moved briskly forward now, very close and personal to her crew, and shot two of her own men in the head, killing both. The second soldier had the briefest instant to reflect in horror upon his mistake to trust these people, but not nearly long enough to act on his mistake. He fell, like the other onto polluted ground, his soul leaving him in an instant. The tall man, duffle bag in hand, and the well-dressed woman moved away through the blackness of the night, leaving the horror and bloodshed in their wake, police and residents of the street, now converging to see what all the fuss was about.

Residents now rushed to the scene of the murders, calling for police and ambulance assistance by mobile phone. Many people were distraught at the sight of the carnage, some too overcome with the bloodshed to try and assist. Others remained, immobile, paralysed with fear, and some thinking that the area remained too dangerous to be in. A few brave, men and women, however, rushed headlong into danger, to see what could be done, only to find that it was too late, all were dead, and the area was again silent, except for the crying of a neighbour and the occasional shriek as people realised the extent of the devastation.

Special police units soon swooped on the area, these were tactical units specially armed with the best of weaponry, full flak jackets, helmets and vests, arriving with sirens blaring, and lights flashing. Immediately, the police began to cordon off the ally way, and the surroundings. After interviewing some individuals, those willing to speak, taking names and addresses, and ushering people back to their homes, and back to bed...not that they would be getting much sleep, this night.

Assistant chief of police, Colonel Kenneth Wong, an aspiring young officer, only 27 years of age, whose mind and eyes were keen, and his demeanour strong and capable, took charge of the murder investigation reporting directly to the chief of police, and through the chief, also to a security council whose job it was to assess national security matters. Kenneth discovered that all six dead were Cambodian nationals, making this seem like a drug deal gone very wrong. But Kenneth wasn't convinced. One of the dead had a vague but believable link to the Americans, if not being covertly employed by the American embassy to do who knows what. This was the first man murdered, Kenneth believed, as he was out the front, and another dead man fell partly on top of him, however, the link to the Americans was vague, nothing that could be shown as even circumstantial evidence...just a few hunches from informants. On the other side, however, two of the soldiers had fairly definite links to the Chinese gangs and by inference, perhaps, to the Chinese presence in Cambodia...but the latter was drawing a long bow. More likely, this was a Chinese gang drug deal gone wrong, as the newspapers had reported. The other party, most likely, taking both the cash and the drugs. *But who was the other party?* Ken wondered.

In the morning, news of a "gang fight" was broadcast on all radio and television stations. The police asked that anyone with pertinent information should come forward, as the police were baffled as to what exactly the situation was. What had happened in that alleyway, leading to the death of six males, was not understood. All were armed and obviously with some specific unknown evil intent. All had tattoos, some many but gang markings were not definite, suggesting that these men were chosen for their anonymity.

Because of the gravity of the situation, the Cambodian nation moved to high alert, doubling security at all airports, embassies, places of worship, and border crossings, into and out of the country, all cargo would be searched, and all travellers and their baggage closely examined. The police wanted answers quickly, before any further disruption to national pride and international standing. When violence and criminal activity took place, the right man for the job was indeed Kenneth Wong, who had already been decorated many times for bravery, intelligent investigative work, an astute mind, and dogged determination. He would investigate fully a crime of any kind, especially when it came to murder!

Chapter 2
Mr Roberts on the Tonle Sap (Siem Reap)

"Mr Roberts, do you have a charter today?" a strong, English, American-accented voice asked. The tall ruggedly built, Cambodian, 34 years of age, hoped that the answer would be a yes, as his family needed the dollars that a good charter job would bring.

At 6 o'clock in the morning, Mr Roberts answered half asleep, lying in his hammock, towards the front of the "Menaka", his just short of 85 feet, motored, charter, and fishing boat, built in the Cambodian style, but also built for speed, and pulling power, having two powerful engines rather than the standard one. "Not at the moment and not many fish around either, so we may as well take the day off. Go home and play with the kids, Vanny." Vanny Hong was disappointed, he needed the money. "Here, Hong, here's six bucks."

"Thanks, brother, I needed that blessing, if only to get through this day." Vanny took the gift reverently in the Cambodian way, with a bow, a smile, and hands clasped together.

Like Roberts, Vanny was a fisherman, *"The salt of the earth"* as the bible would say and lived on the shoreline of the Tonle Sap Lake, he stood six feet three inches tall, tall for a Cambodian but not too unusual these days. He had two children, a boy, and a girl. Roberts by comparison was only five feet and eleven inches tall, but at nearly one hundred kilograms in weight; he was a bulky, seventy-one-year-old man, his hair white and thinning with age, but not balding yet.

Roberts wasn't a naturalised Cambodian, he remained Australian, loyal to the last, a true boy scout. He didn't drink alcohol, he didn't smoke, and he didn't gamble. He did have a few vices though…a little smuggling in the old days, very little fighting, and of course there was the lady, Menaka, and that would classify as womanising, but perhaps it wasn't. He was well-liked by pretty much everyone. Roberts spoke the Khmer language fluently, after spending nearly twenty-five years on and off in Cambodia. It was necessary, however, for him to renew his visa every year to stay in the country. Perhaps, due to his good service, mainly within the Cambodian tourist industry, this year he hoped that he would be offered "free citizenship" rather than having to pay a fortune for it. There were obvious land advantages in being a citizen but, on the whole, Roberts was satisfied as he was, and he wanted nothing more from life, except to work on his fishing boat.

Roberts almost always wore shorts, a t-shirt, socks and sneakers, and a colourful green cap with "Valley of the Giants" written on it. He was a Christian-Buddhist, an odd but workable combination in this Buddhist society. When he became a Buddhist, some of his Christian friends disowned him, it was as if he had a disease and could infect others, hard to do in a country of seventeen million Buddhists. But many friends did not, remaining steadfast. When Roberts went to the temple or the church, or indeed any place of worship, he wore long trousers and good shoes in reverence to the religious atmosphere.

Roberts had some money in the bank but not a fortune, a good tour job and even a little smuggling would keep him afloat in these difficult times. His best opportunity was a good "all day" tour job. As for smuggling, if caught, he could lose his boat and any chance of citizenship and apart from heavy fines, he could spend almost the rest of his life in a Cambodian prison, only to be deported at the end of his incarceration. Hmm, something to think about. But anyway, neither offer seemed to be coming his way anytime soon.

"Mr Robert, you want breakfast?" Nancy said, with a very accented "Cambodian-English", hardly discernible as English but through experience and habit, Roberts knew what phrases and sentences to expect. In any case, she was just practising her English for her imagined trip to the U.S.A. Who knows, it could happen. Nancy was the cook aboard "Menaka" and at 72 years of age, she ruled the galley, and dining area with an iron hand. What she cooked, she served, take it or leave it, no choice here. Having said that, her food was very good and for those who like it spicy, as Roberts did, it was delicious. Roberts always brought sandwiches, milk, biscuits and good coffee and tea, which he served hot, just in case tourists couldn't eat that ever-so-spicy food. Roberts loved spicy food, so for him, there was no problem with the menu.

"No thanks, Nancy, you can stay ashore today, no guests, and I will only take the boat out to warm the engines."

Nancy responded, "You eat that sandwich shit, leftover from four days ago… it's a fridge, not a magic box!" She was right but Roberts only wanted hot tea, and his sugar level this morning was too high anyway. Perhaps he would catch a fish or two, enough for personal use. After some dallying with pots, Nancy moved ashore, and Roberts began to swab the deck before heading out. He was half an hour into that job when a young and very beautiful woman turned up at his mooring.

"Hello."

"Hi," Roberts responded, a slightly intrigued look on his face. *Maybe she was lost?*

"I'm looking for a Mr Roberts, you wouldn't know where I might find him?" Roberts smiled, this could be a little business coming his way.

"I'm Roberts, can I help you with something?" With high heels and a five-star appearance, she didn't look like a fishing or sightseeing tourist.

"I want a man to do a rather important task for me." Roberts smiled again, a large, cheeky grin appearing across his face. He knew that she couldn't mean sex, but he found her words amusing as to all the connotations that could be drawn.

"And what job might that be, may I ask?" Roberts wasn't expecting the reply that came his way.

"I'm looking for someone to take me and a friend, across the border to Vietnam."

"Well," Roberts said, leaning against the boat's rather, fancy railing. "That's not a hard task at all…best way, jump on a plane, and you'll be there within the hour. Bus, less expensive, it'll take a full day though," Roberts, said, seeing his charter drift away on a tide.

"No, it must be by charter boat." Robert's hopes began to be restored.

"Really, that will cost you, it's quite expensive. Across the lake, down the Tonle Sap River to Phnom Penh and then down the Mekong to Vietnam. Quite an adventure for a very young lady."

The lady responded with unusual brevity and no smile, "Yes, quite, will you do it?"

"Just leave your passport and I'll arrange it today."

Again, her response, wasn't as expected, "I can't do that, no passports, no visas, we need to be smuggled down river." Such words came from the lips of a beautiful American woman, almost a Marilyn Monroe look-alike, she was that good-looking.

"Ma'am, you really don't want to do that. Big trouble you know, you could end up spending the next ten years in prison, and for what?" Roberts was beginning to believe that this young girl had a "death wish" or something.

At this point, instead of walking away the girl continued, "My name is Mary, I know you've done this sort of thing before, all I'm asking for is a little help. I need your help, Mr Roberts." Now, there it was, she knew or somehow suspected, that he had smuggled before and yet even the local police didn't know that. Roberts had never been arrested, not even a speeding ticket.

"Sorry, you are mistaken, I don't smuggle anything or anyone. You've got the wrong man. If you want to fish, then I'm your man, tour the Tonle Sap, still your man. But I draw the line at smuggling people."

"I'll be back with an offer, Mr Roberts." Roberts was still calm as he always was, but to be truthful, he was beginning to become just slightly annoyed at the direction of the conversation.

"Don't bother, the answer will still be no." She ignored his words, hopping into a large four-wheel drive, Roberts could not see the number plate, but it was a Toyota, and she drove away. *Well,* thought Roberts, *that's one for the books, a fine lady driving a truck in Siem Reap, where the traffic was murder. She was harder than she looked, this one.*

Chapter 3
On the Loose

"Robert!" Delci a local prostitute, was crying and yelling, calling for assistance. Her message was simple, and this wasn't the first time Roberts had heard this plea. Dolo, a local bully and muscle for the "hundred percent gang" was harassing prostitutes at a brothel and boarding house. Dolo was a young beast, dressed in a suit, with the manners of a pig and an attitude to match his swagger; he was built like a tank and used every bit of his size and weight to advantage. Harassing people, generally meant that he was hitting Menaka, a reformed prostitute well known for her wild and combative ways, and for looking after the girls in this particular bordello. Looking after the girls wasn't her job, she managed the restaurant and bar, for a nice enough, and certainly larcenous character by the name of "Sun Moon", a silly name, but his mother must have loved him to call him that. The prostitutes were "Sun's" girls but "Sun" was afraid of the hundred percent gang, and if it had not been for Menaka, he would have been paying protection money a generation ago. In any case, Dolo approached the girls directly, wanting half of their take. Menaka was protecting the girls, and both the girls and "Sun" reaped the benefits, but the hundred percent gang were becoming more aggressive and Menaka could not help the girls forever, or so Roberts thought.

On arrival, at first, Roberts felt that he might not step into the fray, as Menaka was giving better than she got; pulling Dolo's hair, scratching and tearing at him and his clean suit, turning it into shredded rags. But then things changed and with a single haymaker Dolo brought Menaka to her knees, she was barely conscious, and the next punch would be as deadly as it got.

Roberts stepped in catching Dolo's arm with his own and stopping the forward motion of the blow, which never reached its mark. Roberts then moved to strangle the fight from Dolo, and from behind this was a good plan. Dolo weakened, but suddenly changed position, and he attempted to kick Roberts in the shins. Roberts was too fast, and the kicks didn't work, Roberts applied the choke even more tightly, pulling back, and bringing Dolo to his knees, entirely cutting off Dolo's air supply. For a few seconds, Dolo fought, trying to scratch and punch at Roberts, and then he stopped, his arms dropping to his sides. The choke was perfectly applied. After a time, Roberts released the choke and Dolo fell face first to the ground, directly onto his nose. Blood flowed around his face from a broken nose. Roberts kicked Dolo on his shoulder, for good measure…just a bit of pain for him to remember. His breathing was restored, and he would return to life within ten minutes or less.

Immediately, Roberts took Dolo's wallet, removing several hundred dollars, and he gave this to Menaka. "For the girls and the damages," he said with a friendly smile, throwing the wallet onto Dolo's still-sleeping body. He kept one hundred dollars for his trouble, pocketing the bill with a smile. Most people were smiling at the antics, one guy, a tourist even clapped.

But Menaka looked at Roberts as though her favourite toy had been taken away from her, yelling rather loudly, "You think you are so smart, Roberts? You come in here, big man, big fat bastard, and throw your weight around! I was winning that fight! I had him beat! He knew it too! Go to hell, Roberts, stay out of our business! Okay!" She nodded her head, almost as if she was talking to herself, "Okay," she said.

Roberts calmly smiled, this wasn't the first time Menaka had overestimated her abilities and underestimated her opponent. But that girl had a fire in her belly and wouldn't be cowered. "Well, when he comes around, maybe you can 'talk' him to death, or start another fight." Roberts left with a smile on his face and then he began to laugh loudly, a deep belly laugh, shaking his head and moving down the street at a considerable pace.

Menaka smiled at him as he left, and then realised some people were watching her, so she yelled after Roberts, "Roberts, you come back here and take this sack of shit with you!" She then kicked Dolo once to the ribs as hard as she could; he seemed to feel it and groaned miserably.

*****

The lake was quiet today, Roberts broke the silence as he opened the engines to full throttle. *My God, this boat could move*, he thought. Everything checked out, *"All ship-shape and Bristol fashion"*, was the nautical term, meaning simply his boat was in good order, clean and working well. The boat maintained full throttle for an extended period before he throttled her back to just above idle, and once the engines cooled, he finally turned them off.

Roberts had a very unusual sailing and mast arrangement set up on his motorboat, to take advantage of winds which blew from time to time across the Tonle Sap Lake. Of course, his boat had a shallow draft and couldn't take full advantage of the wind, as a large sailing yacht might do, but still, sails allowed for very quiet, slightly slower, and peaceful travel on the river, at no cost in fuel. He began to raise the masts and then to unfurl the sails…this was really a two-man job if you were in a hurry but Roberts wasn't and today was a good practice at doing the task alone. It was heavy work for one man, but Roberts finished the task in record time.

Steering towards the east home and trailing four fishing lines, he hoped that within the next two hours, he might catch a few fish before the setting of the sun to his west and the final rays of the brilliant sky turned dark. This was the time that Roberts loved best, relaxing, and listening to the gurgle of water against the wooden hull of his boat. He sat at the wheel, and time passed. The sails were in the best of condition, and he couldn't remember a time when his boat was so ready for a voyage. That day he caught nine decent-sized fish. He, Vanny, Nancy and their families would eat well this week, or at least for the next few days.

Roberts returned just a little after dark, having taken down the masts and coming into dock under power, certainly the safer way when travelling alone. He noticed that same Toyota Land cruiser waiting above the dock, with the internal lights on. She was back, and this time she was not alone. As he tied both bow and stern lines, Roberts noticed the two leave the Toyota and since he was familiar with the vehicle, and its height, he deduced the male was over six feet tall. He was handsome but not as young as the girl. He looked a formidable figure, slim, very well dressed and as he and the girl approached, his inferences proved true…he was tall, dark, and handsome.

"Hello, Mr Roberts, we meet again," Mary said, and without mentioning that he had asked her not to return, she continued, "this is my friend, boy-friend to be exact, and he has a proposition for you." *Hmm, was that a fancy way of saying a smuggling job,* he thought.

Roberts was never known for rudeness, and so he answered, "Well, talking is cheap and I have the whole evening ahead of me, so talk." Roberts did not, however, invite them on board, and so they talked standing, the two on the peer and Roberts, now aboard the boat.

The tall guy spoke, with a northern-American accent, "Mr Roberts, I want you to help me get to Cho Tan Chaw, along the Mekong. I want you to do this in an incognito manner." This guy chose his words as vaguely as she did.

"You mean that you want me to smuggle you across the border to Vietnam?" In a still calm and friendly voice, Roberts continued. "Do you realise the consequences for all of us, especially, me, if we get caught?" But somehow, Roberts thought that these two knew exactly what they were doing. "As I said before, there's too much trouble in this for me, and really no reason to do it."

The tall man smiled indulgently, "How about one hundred thousand American dollars for a job that you could pull off with your eyes closed? Roberts, we know how good you can be with this sort of stuff." Roberts was intrigued with the extent of this guy's knowledge, but he didn't even know the guy's name, let alone trust him in the slightest.

"What's your name, anyway?" said Roberts.

"Oh, my apologies," said Mary, "my partner is David Copperfield, a real estate agent from New York, New York."

"You're kidding me right, are you the Dickens' character or the magician?" Roberts didn't mean to be rude, but that is exactly the way it sounded, rude and sarcastic. Roberts apologised, "Sorry, I'm just kidding, I didn't mean to be rude, it was stupid of me."

"No problem," said the tall man, "every asshole says that, oh, just kidding. Didn't mean to call you an asshole." David's sports jacket spread, just enough to reveal an automatic pistol. Roberts' demeanour did not change, but he knew as everybody did, carrying a firearm in Cambodia was a very serious offence. This guy was no real estate agent, and the girl no naïve young thing, just out of preparatory college.

"I'm sorry, no, no deal, I have a business and a lifestyle to protect. Gooday to you." But they didn't leave.

The man spoke, "Mr Roberts, I must confess that I have lied to you. I needed to as my job requires me to do, but I can see that you're an honest man and since, no questions asked, is not working in this case, I am going to tell you the full story." *Sure,* Roberts thought, *need to know, and this guy is going to tell him the full story?*

"Okay, come on board, I'll make tea, and you can jabber to your heart's content. Watch out for that first step." Roberts placed the boarding plank down and they came onboard. They sat on deck at an open table and Roberts put the kettle on a gas stove. "Now, while that boils, we can talk."

The guy complained, "Do you have anything a little stronger, whisky or even a cold beer?"

"No," Roberts replied looking directly into David's eyes. He lied but his alcohol was for paying guests.

"You're a good liar, Mr Roberts, your demeanour tells me that you are telling the truth, but you're not." Roberts didn't mind being caught out by these two, after all this was his boat and his rules. The kettle boiled, Roberts made the tea, and they talked.

Roberts sipped on his hot beverage…heaven, green tea, and guests for the evening. But these two were not really guests, so Roberts figured that he would have to keep his wits about him. The girl was happy with the tea, the guy, not so much. Roberts inquired, "So, what's the story?"

Chapter 4
A Deal with the Devil

David began, "An interesting question, Roberts." The Mister being deliberately left off. "You are or at least you were an Australian operative in Indochina. You were sent on dozens of clandestine missions, all successful, but none of which I could find out anything about. However, you were decorated twice by your government, and for what, I don't know, nobody does. Amongst others, you hold a black belt in karate and a white belt in judo. You box and wrestle or at least you did five years ago. How was that, Roberts? Oh, your name really is Roberts…and that's it, only one name, very unusual." And then David grinned, a smirk rather than a smile.

Roberts wasn't fazed by David's knowledge of him, in fact, most of it was useful, in his characterisation of these two unknown persons.

Roberts sipped his tea, rubbed the stubble on his face, and smiled as if his thoughts had clarified into a clear picture. "I don't have a, err…travel agency to do my groundwork for me," he contemplated, "but, I will see what I can do, with what I have. The fact that you are both Americans means that most likely, you are intelligence operatives from that country, probably C.I.A., otherwise how would you achieve any knowledge of me at all? Secondly, you will act upon my nationalism to try and get whatever it is that you want. And lastly." Roberts pointed at the automatic tucked into David's pants. "Those are illegal in this country, and I presume that you don't have a carry permit for it, nor a gun permit. Oh, and it was three times, I was decorated, three times, not two."

By the look on David's face, Roberts could see that he was correct. Roberts finished his tea, and asked, "What do you two want from me?"

Mary interjected, "We told you, we want you to take us secretly to Vietnam." Roberts brushed his face and shook his head slightly.

"You haven't given me any reason as to why I should do this crazy thing. I'm not impressed by your status, nor do I care for people bringing guns onto my boat."

"Okay, Roberts, here's the story," David began, "two days ago, six men died in a gunfight in Siem Reap." Roberts kept up with the news, no lies so far, David continued, "That meeting was between several agents of the United States. Information on double agents, supposedly working for us, but really working for the Chinese, was to be transferred to the embassy. The point is two double agents escaped with the information in a large satchel. I've received intel that these traitors have gone independent and are heading to Vietnam within a few days, where they will sell the satchel of information to the highest bidder. They will take to the river as the only certain means of getting away. They are being chased by the Chinese, the Russians and of course us. I have been tasked to get back the bag and silence the traitors before they reach Vietnam and are lost forever. They murdered six of our men, it will be my pleasure to end these two. They are well trained, so this will be a dangerous task for everyone, no easy job, and they may have friends." Roberts thought the story plausible, but dealing with the C.I.A. was always dangerous, operatives were well trained, but Roberts was beginning to think that he may come out of this with something.

"Two hundred and fifty thousand, my boat is worth more than twice that, and that would be what I'm risking."

"No, too much, the United States will offer two hundred thousand, if the job is successfully completed."

"And if it is not?"

"Then nothing, Roberts!" David and Roberts looked at one another for what seemed ages but was only a minute, Roberts rubbing his stubble, he needed a shave.

"You'll have to put thirty-five thousand up front as danger money, and another ten if I directly assist you, that's the only way that I'm taking this deal."

"Done!" David said, shaking Roberts' hand. "But the no-guns rule needs to go, and I am told that you have a .38 calibre Smith and Wesson somewhere, I'd be practising a bit if I was you. We will leave tomorrow morning, bright and early."

"Oh," Roberts responded, "and cash, only cash, no government cheques, no bonds, no bitcoin, it's a cash, U.S. dollars deal."

And the deal was struck.

Once they'd left, Roberts immediately called both Nancy and Vanny to explain the situation. Nancy was to stock the boat overnight with plenty of fresh vegetables, fruit, and water. Along with a new supply of cooked food "fish and rice", she would stay at home on this particular charter job. No need for anyone to get hurt or endangered, this was a 'need to know' operation and Nancy was protected by her lack of knowledge.

David was correct, Roberts did have a well-oiled .38 calibre Smith and Wesson pistol, but he thought that this job may take a little more firepower. Vanny was to purchase two 9mm Glocks, three grenades, at least two boxes of 9mm shells and one of .38 Smith and Wesson cartridges, all on the black market, a very costly affair since he wanted the best. Plus a few other items. Roberts paid out thirteen grand overnight, leaving his bank account almost empty. By the time they had finished, the night was almost gone. Soon Mary and David would return and expect to leave; but not before his payment of forty-five thousand U.S. dollars, compliments of the U.S.A.

Nancy wanted to stay on the boat, she knew that Roberts was going to do something dangerous, and she wanted to be of assistance, but he wouldn't allow it and she was sent home. And now, with everything else complete, except refuelling, Roberts explained to Vanny what his role was to be in this business. Vanny would take a Glock, plenty of ammunition and a single grenade. He would ride shotgun on his motorbike from the shoreline, up to but not across the Cambodian/Vietnamese border. He was told that his passengers were not to know of his presence, and thus he could not join too closely with the boat until the job was completed, or if he felt that Roberts was in trouble. "Now, take the boat, refuel it and return. You will carry the forty-five thousand away, immediately distribute it as I have directed and then set out on your journey. The bike is faster, and you will catch us within a single day." Vanny could be relied upon to follow instructions to the letter. Vanny set out to refuel the boat with the money Roberts gave him.

The Toyota turned up only a few minutes after the boat left for refuelling. Roberts met Mary and David at the mooring. "For a minute there, I thought that you had chickened out," said David.

"Now, why would I do that?" said Roberts. "The boat's just gone for refuelling, it will return in about twenty minutes. Now where's that forty-five thousand?"

David was a little peeved, "You'll get your money when I see the boat. You were supposed to be prepared to leave extra early!"

Roberts responded, "Well, it's just after five, the sun hasn't risen yet and if we are going to catch bad guys, plenty of fuel is a must, as we will be under power the whole way. We don't want to be stopping for fuel more than once on this journey. I can wait for the money, or I can count it now, and we can be underway when my man gets back, it's up to you."

Both David and Mary looked about the empty dock suspiciously but finding no sign of a trap, Mary and David, went back to the Land cruiser and collected two cases of luggage and a satchel. David handed the satchel to Roberts saying, "There it is, the upfront forty-five grand, do you want to count it?"

"Of course," Roberts replied, sitting down on the dock he began to count the crisp, new, hundred-dollar bills. Both Mary and David were a little annoyed, watching Roberts count out the cash, but they accepted the situation. It was all there.

Within a few minutes the boat had returned, Mary and David boarded, and Roberts handed the satchel to Vanny. "What about your Land cruiser?" said Roberts.

Without a thought, David threw the keys to Roberts. "Keep it, it's yours, a gift," said David. Roberts thought that the car might be stolen; he gave the keys to Vanny and told him to park it elsewhere, away from anything that may lead to a connection with him or his friends.

Mary interjected, "Mr Roberts, you really are a suspicious man." But Roberts had his reasons, they gave the car away too easily, and outfitted as it was, it would have been worth over sixty thousand. Maybe they had no intention of coming back or having it picked up by someone.

David realised his mistake, he knew that Roberts would infer exactly that, and so he added, "It's a rental, they'll use GPS to pick it up in a day or so. Sorry, I was just joking with you." *Well*, Roberts thought, *that was an intelligent fill-in*. It was dark and Roberts was half-blind, perhaps there was a rental sticker on it, but he hadn't seen one. No surprises there, the blind man doesn't see a rental sticker.

David asked Roberts why his crewman had left, and why the boat was powering so slowly, at less than half throttle. Roberts explained that his crew of one did not need to be in danger, that he wouldn't be of much help and so he was sent home to bank the money and get rid of the Land cruiser. As for the speed, this boat was the fastest on the lake and going faster than this would immediately draw suspicion. If their enemy was on the lake and ahead of them, they would catch them, if they were behind them, Roberts would find out from friends on the river and they would know.

Chapter 5
Romance of the River

Now David was satisfied, and he and Mary retired to one of two luxurious, air-conditioned cabins below deck and were not heard from for hours. *Now, what could they be up to?* Roberts thought with a big smile. *Maybe they were tired and needed a good sleep,* he thought, *More likely they were enjoying that big bed.*

Menaka had a luxury captain's cabin, a wheelhouse, and a full kitchen above deck, along with plenty of room to fish and see the sites, tables, and chairs with a view, for meals and a fish hold for the odd occasions when Menaka had a big catch.

After some time, Mary and David returned above deck, showered and in bathing gear...much more suited to these climates. Both bodies were perfect knockouts, she was an incredible beauty in a tight, skimpy costume that didn't leave much to the imagination. He was a Greek Adonis, in loose-fitting board shorts, muscled from head to toe, tall, lean and incredibly handsome, *Move over James Bond!* he thought, with long dark hair he would be sure to thrill the girls. Mary and David kissed, and Roberts felt the need to look in a different direction but since they were directly in front of him, this was a little difficult.

She had no morality when it came to this man. As they kissed, her hand drifted towards his cock within his board shorts and she stroked and caressed it a few times. Perhaps she just had no morality with anyone, maybe it was all an act? David looked towards Roberts with a smile. "Got to love it, old man!" he said kissing her just once on the forehead. They stopped fondling.

"Any news, Roberts, from your friends on the river?" David sat in the shade on a deck chair. Mary joined him, on his lap.

"No, so I am guessing that your friends will be behind us, and still on the lake. Do you want me to slow down, so that they can catch up to us?"

David answered, "No, just in case they are ahead of us, we could perhaps increase speed a little bit. We can always turn back to catch them if they're behind us. In any case, they're not my friends!"

Roberts informed them of their position on the lake, "We will leave the lake soon enough, and enter the Tonle Sap River, which leads to Phnom Penh. By then it will be dark, but enjoy the setting sun, while you can. Once in the waters of the river you will need to stay hidden, I have a secret compartment below deck which I have used on occasions to smuggle goods across the border. Once concealed, it is very hard to find. The police along the river know me, and unless they see you, they won't search the boat. That won't be true from the Mekong all the way to Vietnam, all of those guys are deadly serious, and I don't have a friend among them."

Mary and David enjoyed a romantic time, watching the setting sun, and cuddling, and they finally retired to their cabin to do what all young couples do when they have the time and the romantic inclination. All reports came back by mobile from friends that Roberts had living along the shoreline, some were smugglers, others were police but mostly they were fishermen living on the river…no one behind his boat and no one ahead either. It seemed that this mission may well turn out easier than Roberts had imagined, but then he wouldn't collect another cool quarter of a million dollars. To be truthful, Roberts was satisfied with the peaceful life on the river.

Vanny phoned Roberts at one in the morning, he said that he had caught the Menaka by 11 pm and was following the boat ever since. Roberts knew there was more to this story, otherwise, Vanny would have simply texted A.O.K. or something to that effect. "Mr Roberts, there are two dark, black, trucks following your boat from the shoreline. Each has three good men, that's six men, Mr Roberts. What have you gotten yourself into?" Roberts didn't answer, it was 'need to know', and Vanny was safer not knowing. Roberts asked for and was supplied the number plates, from both vehicles. Vanny had been close to those vehicles, too close for Roberts' comfort, and he ordered Vanny to give the two vehicles and the men in them, a wide berth. Vanny said okay, and the conversation ended.

Roberts didn't wake the two lovers but once the night was as dark as it was going to get, he turned all the lights out and throttled down the engines to a crawl, heading for the opposite bank where the tracks were very difficult to unpassable, and fishermen reported no strange activity on the roads or the tracks. Roberts knew that one car would stay where they lost sight of Menaka and the other would continue downstream at a slower pace, trying to pick up the trail once more. Menaka couldn't outrun the cars, but why were they being followed anyway? Was it the Chinese, or the Russians? If it was, then they were following David in the hope that he would lead them to that satchel of information. Roberts was quite familiar with C.I.A. procedures, but couldn't recollect an occasion where lists of double agents would be passed by hand, but that could be true, maybe? If it were not true, these agents could be after something else. Roberts wondered what that might be.

Best call a young police friend, Kenneth Wong, who owed Roberts a couple of favours and find out who these guys in the trucks were. By now it was very late, two in the morning, but security matters were, after all, very important. Roberts phoned Kenneth who was fast asleep at the time and after several minutes Roberts got a response, "What the fuck do you want, Roberts, it's after two in the morning! This better be good!"

"Well, I want you to run two sets of plates for me, Ken, this is urgent otherwise I wouldn't ask." Roberts gave him the plates by SMS, adding, "Can't tell you anything else, except, it's 'need to know'. Please do this for me, ASAP, Ken, I need this information. It's a top priority."

Roberts disconnected, giving Ken no time to ask questions. He knew that Ken would be interested to figure out what he was up to. Less than two hours later, Ken phoned back. "So what's the word, Ken," said Roberts.

"The word tells me that you are into some 'deep shit', Roberts, those plates were hundred percent gang. What's this all about?" Kenneth's voice wasn't tired anymore, he was excited as if he was a hound after a fox.

Roberts didn't answer what the matter was about, but he did give his approximate location, "I'm on the Tonle Sap, about halfway down river towards Phnom Penh, there are at least six guys in those two cars following my boat from the shoreline. If you want to know something about the laneway killings, I'd arrest and question them, if I was you." Ken was no one's puppet, but arresting and questioning bad guys was his job.

"You're not going to tell me anything more, are you? Okay, Roberts, I'll get them off your tail, but I'm on to you. Don't expect mercy when I catch you doing, whatever it is that you're doing."

David rose by 4:30 am, he wore nothing but his boxer shorts when he bolted from below deck, and he wasn't pleased. "What's going on, Roberts? The boat has stopped, and we are near the left shore."

"The Port shore," Roberts corrected.

But David was angry, and perhaps a little drunk. "Don't smart ass me Roberts, just answer the questions."

Roberts drew back in the deck chair that he was sitting in. "Okay, I'll explain my actions, and then when you are fully awake, you can take the watch till seven thirty and I'll sleep for a bit, after all, I've been awake for nearly forty hours, while you two have been, 'sleeping'." Roberts smiled at the 'sleeping' comment, but David didn't pick up on the sarcasm or if he did, he chose to ignore it. "While you were asleep, I got a report from villagers and fishermen that we were being followed from the shoreline by some guys in a truck. Well-known hundred percent gang members. Anyway, we can't outrun them, so we need to outthink them. It's like a game of chess, we're the pawns, and they're the rooks or something like that."

David was still angry, "What? Are you altogether up to this job, Roberts? Maybe you're just too old or too stupid." Roberts didn't allow people to disrespect him, and certainly not this guy.

"My boat, my rules, you can have your pistol, but I'm the captain and you're the passenger. Is that clear?" David didn't seem impressed, but he didn't say anything. "One question," Roberts asked it before David could say no, "why are we being followed by the largest gang in Cambodia?"

David gave a reasonable answer, "Maybe they're working for the Chinese or the Russians, maybe they want to sell the list themselves, I don't know." David took the watch.

Roberts got up and went to his cabin. He locked the door, and opened the safe, taking out the .38 and the Glock. He loaded both, placing a large quantity of shells in both pockets. .38s in the right and 9mm shells in the left. He placed the .38 in the front of his pants and the Glock behind his back. He drew on his jacket to cover both and slipped into a small smugglers' passage within his boat.

Chapter 6
Mary Loses Her Cool, While Kenneth Plays Catch Up

David woke Roberts at exactly 7:30 am, as Roberts had asked him to do, and immediately, Roberts pulled the stern and bow anchors. He started the engines at an idle, heading for the middle of the river. Once he was in deep water, he set the speed to low, placed on the wheel lock, and served breakfast. During breakfast, Roberts required only one correction to the heading and not needing to watch over the boat's path, he spent all of his time serving and eating. Mary had already risen. She was wearing a skimpy shawl, over different bikini pants, bra, and an elegant pair of high heels. She looked like every man's dream of a perfect, "*Bond Girl*", right down to the nail polish; toes and fingers, all painted a dazzlingly red. Roberts offered to serve her first. "Tea or coffee, Mary?"

"Tea, if you please, Mr Roberts." Roberts didn't give much of a choice with breakfast, but it was hearty and delicious if he did say so himself. Slightly spiced vegetables, fried eggs done as you preferred, a rash of bacon, spiced fish and rice, fruit of several exotic kinds, bread rolls, margarine, and coffee or tea.

"And, David, what would you prefer?"

"I would prefer a whisky and soda, is that possible?"

"Sorry, David, not on the menu. What you drank last night was up to you, but today you'll need your wits about you. No doubt, at some point this morning, we are going to have a visit from the police. At that time, you will be ashore, on our port side," Roberts pointed the direction, "using a motorised dingy to travel the five kilometres downstream. You'll go to the river house that I stipulate, and I will pick you up from there. The house is four metres above the waterline, on stilts, so it's a bit of a climb, you can't miss it, it's entirely on its own, and it's painted blue. It belongs to me and is presently deserted, I checked with a local who was there only a few hours ago."

"I can't swim Mr Roberts," said Mary, a strange, concerned, look on her face, and a single tear developing in one eye.

"What?" Roberts looked surprised, maybe she wasn't C.I.A. as they had said, *"I can't swim"*.

David was upset at the statement, roughly interjecting, "Doesn't matter, you're in a boat for God's sake!"

Mary wasn't reassured by David's bluster. "Can't I be concerned? After all, it's my life that I'm risking." Roberts felt a degree of pity for her. To his knowledge, all trained C.I.A. agents would know how to swim extremely well. He'd never met one who could not. As for David, he wasn't pleased about her gaffe, but he couldn't shut her up without some form of incident, and so he looked uncomfortable, to say the least.

Roberts answered, "Don't worry, Mary, I'll make certain that you're wearing a life jacket, and you will float irrespective of your ability to swim. But those high heels and shawl will have to be replaced by more appropriate jungle attire. I hope you have that in that suitcase of yours?" She did, but for the next half hour as David and Mary re-dressed, there seemed to be a frost in the air between the two lovers. David gave her no sign of affection; it seemed that the love affair was over.

She asked about snakes and sharks but was assured that there were no sharks and very few dangerous snakes in the river. Roberts summed her up as one tough cookie, but not a C.I.A. agent. When she and David returned, properly attired, both wore a Glock sidearm. "If you must wear a sidearm, cover them up," warned Roberts, "otherwise, even a fisherman will report you." They both readjusted the Glocks, tucking them securely behind their backs. She was not unfamiliar with a pistol, making certain that the safety was on before hiding it in her belt and putting on the life jacket that Roberts had supplied.

Still, David did not look happy. However, without complaint, he and Mary moved to the dinghy and headed at the full outboard throttle, down river. With their permission, Roberts had stowed all of their gear in hidden compartments on his boat. Not a sign of them could be found. He fixed the bedding, did the breakfast dishes, and placed every dish away as if it had never been used. Within a few minutes, a police power boat came along the starboard side, ordering Roberts to stop and be boarded. Warning shots pelted the water only a metre in front of his boat. He immediately brought his boat to a stop, from slow. Several police officers with submachine guns jumped aboard and Kenneth was last to cross to Roberts' boat. "Were those shots really necessary, Ken?" said Roberts.

Ken responded with a smile, "No, but I do like to make a point when dealing with you, Roberts." The police had already searched Roberts' person for any sign of contraband, drugs, weapons, or large sums of money. They found nothing. They were thorough, but Roberts more so in his clean-up.

"Okay, what are you up to, Roberts?" Kenneth had already arrested the gang members, questioned them, and placed them in prison until he was satisfied that no laws had been broken. When arrested, they were found to be unarmed except for a couple of hatchets in the back of each truck. They had immediately claimed police harassment, but this was Cambodia, not the U.S.A., and Ken had arrested them on suspicion of something, and he didn't really care what.

"Well, those guys were following my boat and I figured that they meant to do me harm, so I phoned a friend."

Ken smiled, and spoke in Khmer to his officer, "*Check the boat from bow to stern, find something.*" His men fanned out checking everything from the teapot to the toilet. Kenneth continued in Khmer, "*Roberts, what are you doing on the river?*"

Roberts responded, "*Well, there was no work in Siem Reap, it must be a COVID thing, and so, I thought I would try Phnom Penh, maybe there would be more work there?*" Kenneth knew that he was lying but Roberts' premise was a good one.

"*And why should the hundred percent gang be after you?*"

"*I sort of hurt one of them, a little bit, in Siem Reap. Maybe, they were looking for revenge?*" said Roberts, trying to look as innocent as he could, but Roberts never looked innocent, some people never do. However, payback by the hundred percent gang was a reasonable excuse, and it went down well enough. At least for the moment, it seemed plausible enough. But Ken didn't really buy it…he kept a poker face that could not be read.

"I will hold them for twenty-four hours, Roberts. I'll question them again, and then I will let them go. Is that clear, Roberts?"

"Crystal clear, that should be long enough," Roberts answered, a smile on his face.

"You know that I'll get you, one of these days, my friend. You'll slow up, make a wrong move, and that will be the end."

"Everything ends brother, hopefully, I will be around for a little bit longer. Do you want a game of Khmer chess before you go, Ken? I haven't had a good game in a while."

"*We found gun powder residue on your boat, Roberts.*"

"*Well then, don't be using machine guns near Menaka, next time,*" Roberts said, with a smile. Kenneth left without the game of chess, feeling that he had already missed a major move. He would observe this game more closely but at a distance.

When Roberts picked Mary and David up at the river house, Mary was crying. Her sadness did not seem to stem from her inability to swim. Roberts wondered what had caused her unhappiness.

After storing the dingy, they were underway again, but now Roberts demanded that they hide and stay hidden till nightfall. It would be a hard day for both passengers but not so uncomfortable as to necessitate any relaxation of this rule.

Chapter 7
'You Snooze, You Lose'

After only two hours, Mary seemed to wilt, hiding in one of the secret compartments. She began to whimper, and Roberts having heard enough pulled them both from the compartment and sat them on the bed. "Stay here in the room, if you like, or come upstairs for a short time, you can have a shower, or watch TV but try to keep as quiet as you can, or we're all done for. I'll tell you when you must get back in the hide." Roberts procrastinated, but he had relented, and his rule relaxed for a beautiful woman. They both chose to come upstairs, and Roberts hoped that he would not regret it. Mary was thankful but David, as usual, found fault in Roberts' attitude.

"Why don't we just give her a shot and put her to sleep until we reach Phnom Penh harbour that would be the safe move?" Roberts gave David a look that said, *you really are pathetic*, but he said nothing, returning to the wheelhouse.

"But," said Roberts, "you have at least an hour before you need to hide, so enjoy the scenery while you can."

David sipped on his coke can, while Mary sat at a table with a pot of tea. She looked to Roberts like a goddess…all curves, and so much of it showing. A bikini, covered with a thin, silk, full-length slip, slippers upon her feet and a large blue hat to match. She wore dark sunglasses which only added to her mystery. Roberts continued to steer Menaka down the river.

"You're an old man, Roberts, still walking around with an out-of-date weapon. Most people gave up on that pistol in the seventies, even the police." Roberts said nothing, and so David dug a little deeper into the enigma that was Roberts. "I know that you still have that .38, somewhere, it's an old police weapon, yeah." David wasn't expecting a response, to his statement.

Roberts shrugged his shoulders and continued to steer the boat. "They're a tough little weapon, and it fits in my pocket more easily than your Glock."

"The word was that you used to be pretty good with that .38, Roberts. But that was over thirty years ago. Do you keep it clean? Are you still good with it?" David looked at Roberts's eyes, questioningly. But Roberts showed little reaction.

And then, Roberts partially lied, "Probably not, but I could get lucky, I suppose?"

David was not impressed with the response, "There's no such thing as luck, Roberts, you know that, one in the head, right between the eyes, and two to the body just to make sure! That's the way they taught us! But it was said that your method was always two to the body, followed sometimes by one to the head…that's very different, why? Was that because you're half blind, Roberts?"

Roberts didn't like the rude way that he was being questioned and analysed, but he wasn't falling for David's techniques, but he did correct the eye weakness issue, "That's legally blind from birth, not half blind." And he smiled for effect.

Unexpectedly, David threw his coke can into the air and over the side of the boat, he drew his weapon and placed three shots in succession, each shot made the can spin higher and further from the boat. Mary didn't move from her chair, she seemed uninterested or perhaps disconnected from the reality of David's violence. Maybe she had seen this trick before, or worse?

"Well, what do you think?" David asked. Then he added, "Mary can do better, but not by much." He smiled at her, and she returned the kindness with a most beautiful look.

Even though Roberts had killed seventeen men, the reality was that he didn't like killing people, so shooting them in the body seemed an option during his years within the secret service. Of course, more often, he'd shot people in the arms and legs…a very unusual approach considering that some were supposed to be, *"Removed with extreme prejudice"*, which was the term used for murder, in the day. But Roberts had never murdered anyone. The seventeen confirmed kills were due to attacks on him and his friends. His .38 had never misfired or jammed, and his method of shooting was to wait till his enemy was in his 'sweet spot' and then he could shoot, almost without aiming his weapon.

David was fast, fast with the Glock, and accurate, too. If it ever became necessary, Roberts wondered if he could win against such an opponent. No doubt his unarmed combat skills were just as impressive, maybe even more so. David was one hell of a dangerous man, in the prime of his manhood.

An hour later, as Menaka approached the Port of Phnom Penh, Roberts received a call on the marine radio ordering him to dock for a customs inspection. This was slightly unusual but within the parameters of normal operating procedures. He wondered, *Was this Ken's doing or another party?* He ordered Mary and David to hide, checked that all was well, and continued the journey to the dock. A marine police boat followed him into the dock...*Okay, not normal operating procedures. Someone had ordered this search.*

The search was thorough, Ken was not present, and this time the police spoke only Khmer. A high-ranking officer, a captain, seemingly leading the customs check was rude to the point of hatred. When asked if he had people on board, Roberts responded '*No*' and was immediately slapped across the ear and side of his face with an open hand. Considerable pain and a humming reverberated through his head, he wondered, *Has my eardrum burst?* He knew that his left eardrum had burst, a trickle of blood leaving his ear. With his left ear, he could hear nothing at all, and a headache set in quickly. As usual, Roberts remained calm, wiping blood from the side of his face with a clean handkerchief.

Roberts smiled, a cheeky look of disrespect upon his face but he said nothing. The officer asked again, and again Roberts said '*No*'. Again the officer struck out towards the other ear, but this time Roberts blocked the blow. They looked at one another, defiantly. Roberts said in Khmer, "*Please do not do that, as I only have one left.*" The officer said, in a totally controlled Khmer voice, his hand still being held by Roberts, "*I want David and the money.*"

Roberts looked at him, with what he hoped was a look of puzzlement and said, "*What money, and who's David?*"

A police corporal reported, "*There is nothing on the boat, sir.*" He saluted and waited. The commanding officer contemplated the situation for a moment. He rubbed the back of his head and said, *"This boat is ordered to stay in dock for the next twenty-four hours. You cannot leave the boat for any reason, Roberts."* Then abruptly he left, taking his men with him. But the officer placed a police guard, armed with a submachine gun on the dock to watch over the boat.

Roberts waited ten minutes and then got Mary and David from the hide. He filled them in on the happenings. David was ropable. "We can't stay on this boat…tonight they'll come for us."

Mary seemed even more concerned than David. "Mr Roberts, David is correct, tonight they'll come, and they may even sink your boat, with us in it."

Still, Roberts seemed unconcerned. "Who will come for us, David, and why would they attack my boat? After all, they need you alive to find these guys with the satchel, remember?" David considered Roberts' argument.

"Look, Roberts, I think these guys, Chinese, Russians, or crooks, or whoever they are, are finished following us. They will attack the boat tonight. If we're not on it they'll go away, otherwise…is there any way that we can leave without being noticed?" Roberts thought, *These two are cool characters, I'll go along with their arguments for the moment.*

"Yes, there is a way, on and off the boat without being seen, but it's difficult."

"How difficult?" questioned Mary.

"For you, as difficult as it gets…night diving at a depth of more than two metres for about a quarter of a kilometre, followed by a climb up three metres onto a peer, and then back again when we are certain that it's safe." Mary began to cry, all pretence of hardness gone. For her, this was scary stuff.

"Alright stay on your own and be murdered," David said, "just go to sleep and they'll be here soon enough!" She cried, and sobbed, a little louder.

Roberts placed his arm around her shoulders, saying, "I know that this will be difficult for you, being that you can't swim, and honestly, night diving is scary enough as it is, without any extra problems, but I'll hang on to you the whole way. I will not leave your side. You may be scared, but honestly, if you close your eyes I will lead you the whole way, and you can relax, just like at a spa. In fact, you can pretend that this is a 'spa adventure'. Before you know it, we'll have finished…then back again for another adventure. Then we're done, we can sleep the rest of the night in peace." The 'spa adventure' analogy seemed to do the trick and she quietened.

David didn't seem the slightest bit interested in what he was being told, but Roberts hoped he had night diving skills and was up to the job. Both David and Mary had wrapped their weapons tightly, in plastic foil, their intention to be armed made very clear. Roberts left his .38 in the gun locker and the Glock and grenades were hidden where they would not be found. *So far,* Roberts thought, *David had proven to be a muscle-bound, self-centred, arrogant, prick with little or no interest in the welfare of his partner. Well,* Roberts thought, *I think that I just summarised the average C.I.A. agent.* But Roberts thought again, *I must not underestimate my opponent if I snooze, I will lose.*

By now, Roberts was once again sorely in need of sleep. But with little hope of a snooze any time soon. He could feel his strength waning, but his spirit remained strong. The scuba gear was stowed in the forward bulkhead, but he would bring all the gear to the second cabin below deck. There they would suit up for the dive, then head out using a watertight doorway, below the waterline. No one would observe their exit. The guard would not see bubbles, Roberts hoped, as the water was dark and the night blackening fast.

*****

David headed straight for the peer in the direction Roberts had stipulated, he had no problem whatsoever… David knew as much about night diving, it seemed, as Roberts himself. But he did not stick around to aid Mary through her difficulties, that task was left entirely to Roberts. Roberts was already exhausted, his eardrum ached, but he had a considerable task in front of him. *Come on, Roberts, get with it, man!* he said to himself, still displaying the calm that he hoped would be infectious, and that Mary would not panic during this dangerous dive. If she did, this could be the end for both of them.

It soon became obvious that she was terrified, and he would have to drag her the entire way; her eyes tightly closed and her body limp. She didn't even kick to assist forward movement. She was doing her best not to lose control of herself; she was a brave girl. Roberts thought, *At least she's not fighting me, for that would be a disaster*. The distance seemed an eternity, Roberts resting every twenty metres or so and checking his compass; she lay quietly, but for Roberts, she was dead weight, and his exhaustion seemed endless. Eventually, they made it to the correct peer 250 metres away. David did assist them in climbing the jetty and within a few minutes, they were removing their diving gear. David had removed his gear well before Roberts's arrival. All the gear was stowed behind large oil drums, and they waited and watched.

An hour passed without incident and then two modern, black, four-wheel drives turned up. Eight men, they were not police, but a mercenary, tactical response team perhaps, due to their weapons and dress. They entered the dock and spoke to the police guard, who seemed to have expected them, as he received a mobile call only a minute before their arrival. He pointed at the boat and said something. Roberts couldn't hear anything that was being said, probably not due to the slap on his ear, but rather the distance that they were away. The soldiers entered the boat, their lights flashing about. For fifteen minutes, nothing much happened, but it was obvious that they were searching for Roberts and any other sign of life. They found nothing, and then the soldiers left the boat and spoke again with the guard. Roberts could see that the guard was arguing with them, and though Roberts used binoculars, he could not see individual faces, they were wearing masks and it was just too dark to catch a glimpse of a face.

The guard was forced to kneel, more arguing ensued, and then he was shot in the head. His body was picked up and tossed off the dock and into the river. Roberts felt sorry for the man, but what could he do? The military unit got back into the vans and drove away. David commented, "That could have been us." The murder of a police officer had changed everything. When the officer was found in the river, the following morning, most likely Roberts would be arrested and his boat impounded. Another search of his boat would be inevitable, but if the police officer's body was not found then perhaps, they would let him go. To be assured of this, Roberts had a plan B; like a game of chess, Roberts always had another plan, and another move.

"Okay," Roberts said, "we need to change tack here, if we don't, we're done for. I will send both of you to a safe house in Phnom Penh. Your driver is a friend of mine and you will be safe with him. I will move the boat ten kilometres or so downstream if they let me go."

David became very agitated, "Oh no, you're not leaving us in some house while you run back to Siem Reap! You don't think that I'm stupid do you?"

"A little bit," said Roberts. Before David could complain or respond he went on, "Look, I'm not leaving you, but if I don't get rid of that guard's body, then tomorrow we're all finished. The boat will be searched again, and you can't remain on board. This way, at least we have a chance of getting you to Vietnam. But you've got to do it my way, okay!" David nodded his head in acceptance.

Roberts moved off and well away, to make his mobile call, he spoke only Khmer. He phoned a friend, a tuk-tuk driver by the name of 'James Ly'. He used James exclusively for the most dangerous missions. James would be armed as he always was with a hatchet in the tuk-tuk and a knife hidden in his belt. James had military training and was an excellent kick boxer. He offered James ten thousand dollars to take these two to a safe house and watch over them. He would then deliver them downstream to one of several locations…James knew the job well. Hide, protect, and move as necessary. The offer was accepted, and Roberts sent his location via a smuggler's burner phone. Roberts gave James enough of a background for him to understand that these two were not friends of his but quite likely, evil business partners and were not to be trusted. Doing anything with them would be dangerous. He then called Vanny and asked him to watch over the driver and his cargo. Vanny reported that he was no more than two hundred metres away and that he already had the three in his line of sight.

Roberts began to get back into his diving gear when James turned up. James had been asked to speak Khmer only, to listen carefully to anything that David or Mary may say, and to report back to Roberts as soon as he could. Mary and David jumped into the tuk-tuk, which sped away, the driver already knowing everything that he needed to do.

It took Roberts nearly three hours to stow the extra diving gear away, to find the body of the policeman floating in the river, and to attach the body by two ropes to a large rock at a depth of six metres, almost four hundred metres from his boat. If for any reason the body came loose, it would float down the river and into the Mekong current, where hopefully it would not be discovered for at least a few days. By now Roberts was facing complete exhaustion and he could only dream of Mary and David, deep in sleep at the safe house, where they had been for nearly three hours…sleeping.

Chapter 8
Bad Times and Bad Blood

Earlier that night, on the peer with Roberts, David, and Mary.

In two suitcases, David had stashed just over five million American dollars. The money was well hidden on Roberts' boat, but David surmised, that Roberts was too smart not to have realised that something very valuable was in those cases. He had every reason to believe that Roberts had already seen the money and was waiting for his best opportunity to run. Unlike Mary, David always checked his weapon, at least once a day. He had found the blanks in the magazine…the first bullet had been real to cover the rest. *It was likely,* he thought, *that Roberts wanted the money for himself and would abscond as soon as he could do so.* But, David figured, that Roberts would stick around since he still believed that David was C.I.A., and working for the American government.

If anything went wrong at this point, David thought, *Roberts would believe the U.S. government would think that he had something to do with stealing the money.* David calculated that Roberts would smuggle him across the border, and when they were clear of Cambodian law, Roberts would attempt to kill both him and Mary.

He believed that Roberts was bright enough to devise such a fiendish plan. Roberts would kill him, perhaps as soon as a kilometre into Vietnam waters. Now David had another thought; Mary had been nothing but trouble since their romantic time on the boat. And, she would collect her share of five million dollars or perhaps be killed by Roberts? In any case, better to get rid of her now and end her troublesome ways.

David had decided to kill Mary as soon as he could but first he thought, one more night with that brilliant body, one more passionate remembrance of her heavenly scent, his cock deep in her pussy. He decided that she would be a loss after all, but he would make it quick, she would never know that she had been shot, or that she had been betrayed. He had employed her, very successfully, to commit several murders for him but really, except for her pistol shooting, and her obvious other talents, she was rather naïve.

A tuk-tuk arrived, and Roberts introduced James as a good man who would look after both of them. He would stay with them at the safe house and then, deliver them to the appropriate rendezvous, the following day or at the latest, the day after that, if things were a little difficult. James drove at a speed consistent with the law, mostly under 48 kilometres per hour, through otherwise deserted roads at one thirty in the morning. By two o'clock, they were at the safe house, and David and Mary went straight upstairs to bed. James stayed inside the house, but downstairs; he tried to report to Roberts without any success. Vanny had followed them, on his motorbike, as directed and he stayed outside and watched.

David and Mary were having the time of their young lives; to the point that David even reconsidered his actions; but no,

Mary would be a continual risk, a risk that was better closed off here and now.

He waited until he had cum for the third time; she was satisfied after the second, but he needed that extra boost, and he got it. "Wow," he said to Mary, "you've learned a lot since we've been together. I think I'm in love!" She responded with a kiss to his lips and then she rolled over and slept. When David was certain that Mary was in deep sleep, he picked up his Glock from beside the bed, covered the weapon with a small blanket and then his pillow, and shot.

The time was nearly four o'clock in the morning when the single shot splintered the air. In the quiet, the shot was relatively loud but didn't disturb a sleeping neighbourhood. James and Vanny were, however, awake and on guard. Both heard the shot and James, with a hatchet in his left hand, raced upstairs to see what had happened. Vanny waited, with both a Glock tucked into his trousers and a grenade in his left pocket, nervously for a report, he would wait no longer than a few minutes, and then he would go in. He tried to contact Roberts but with no response.

By the time James had reached the top of the staircase, David had turned on a light and covered Mary's body with a blanket. With Glock in hand, David faced James. David said, almost casually in English, "She was a double agent, I caught her contacting the Chinese." James understood what David had said, but he didn't believe him, but against an automatic pistol, what could he do? For now, James accepted that discretion was the better part of valour, and thus avoided a dangerous situation which probably would not have gone his way. James said nothing but David had already decided that he knew some English and had understood what he had been told.

James contacted Vanny, who was still outside and briefly told him the story. Vanny responded by trying to contact Roberts by phone, this time he got through, telling Roberts what he had been told. "Do you believe that shit, Roberts?" Vanny said, in Khmer.

"Not on your life!" said Roberts. "But we will go along with it for now, brother."

"In any case," said Roberts, "you can't stay there anymore. Go and get David and James and move them to a new location." He gave an address that was free of video surveillance. A location that had many entrance and exit profiles...Roberts didn't want this murder to turn into a lifetime struggle, with police tracking him forever. Already this deal had turned from bad to worse. And he knew that the next step would be the confiscation of his boat, irrespective of any crime that he may or may not have committed. With less than an hour of sleep, Roberts' mind was swimming in a sea of doubt.

*****

At Police Headquarters, minutes after the Policeman was shot dead.

Captain Poc knew that the policeman was dead, it was Captain Poc who led the mercenary team to search Roberts' boat, and he personally killed the officer who had failed him. Poc had decided that David must have left the boat before the hundred percent gang mercenary hit squad had arrived. *At that time of night,* Poc thought, *David would need a tuk-tuk, a car, or a bike to make his escape.*

Poc reported to his police superiors that his policeman was no longer responding to requests and thus all main road video was to be searched for any suspicious behaviour. In fact, he was looking for a means of finding and killing David and grabbing the five million American dollars. At that time of the night, the docks, especially the impound docks, were all but empty, and Poc found, on video, what he was looking for. Two people entered a tuk-tuk, close to the impound docks, and the driver moved off. Someone, maybe Roberts, lurked behind them at a distance. Poc couldn't see the required detail in order to track down the driver, but he knew exactly which cameras in the region would film the driver's further movements. He ordered the immediate confiscation of these videos.

By four o'clock, he had identified three tuk-tuks with number plates that may fit his description. For these drivers, he had used phone location finding to look at their movements. Only one tuk-tuk had turned off his phone for an hour or so, and later the driver's phone had been used several times without success to contact someone.

Poc knew that he had his man, and it was likely that David would be found at the same location, perhaps with five million American dollars. This made him very happy; soon he would be a very rich man. He reported to the hundred percent gang's superior, who gave him the go-ahead to kill David and get the money. The superior's nephew had died in that alleyway in Siem Reap, so the money was only of secondary importance to him. But to Poc, the money was everything, and he would torture David and Roberts until he had it.

Captain Poc left the police headquarters to meet his assault team, most were not policemen but mercenaries. He was very pleased with himself. Today he would kill David and with any luck get all the money. Then he would arrest and torture Roberts just to see the look on Roberts's face when he beat him senselessly. Then Roberts would go to a Cambodian prison forever. *Maybe,* he thought, *he could even buy Roberts' boat at a bargain price!* Poc was extremely satisfied, *Today would be a good day!* he thought.

The team suited up and jumped into the black four-wheel drives. Eight mercenaries ready to torture and kill at their boss's request. They headed for the location of the tuk-tuk that would lead them to David.

Chapter 9
The Getaway of the Three

After four o'clock, at the safe house, minutes after Mary's murder.

Vanny phoned James and told him of the change of plans, he crossed the road and knocking at the door, was allowed in. David, who had already dressed, was surprised to see Vanny again, but James knew Vanny was watching.

"You are Roberts's man! I thought Roberts said that you wouldn't be coming?"

Vanny responded, "Mr Roberts wants you moved to another location now. We need to go!"

David wasn't thinking quickly but, drawing his Glock, he levelled it at Vanny, and said, "I'm in charge here, I say where we go, and when! Now, empty your pockets." Vanny drew the Glock from the back of his trouser belt, and gently placed it upon a coffee table. "I said, your pockets!" David commanded. Vanny took the grenade and placed it on the table next to the pistol. "What? Roberts wanted you to blow me up?" David said, in a loud, sarcastic, but rather fearful voice.

"No man! I'm your protection, don't be silly. You just committed a murder, you got to get out of here!"

"Maybe, but I'll just take these to insure my continued good health." David placed the second Glock in his belt and the grenade into his pocket. No sooner had he done so, Poc and his mercenaries parked on either side of the street, a few metres from the tuk-tuk and a dozen metres from the house where the three were located. The only other sign of life in the street was an old woman, walking her dog, as she did every morning at this time. David's house was the only one in the street with lights on inside.

"That'll be it!" Poc said in Khmer. "Do your job! I want them alive, especially David." Each man had a picture of the woman and David, each man knew his job. The team wore tactical radio, and one team began to move towards the back of the house while Poc's team, with Poc leading, waited at the front, would breach the front door. On Poc's command, both teams entered simultaneously. The second commander found it strange that the back door was unlocked, but before he could comment on his findings, a 9mm bullet struck him in the head. A second struck him to the body vest, but he was already dead. A second man fell almost instantly, a headshot stealing his life away. Things at the front of the house were worse for Poc's team. David had rigged the grenade to the front door and placed a can of fuel at the location, spreading a little of the gas around, but not enough to be smelt from outside. If Poc had been careful, perhaps he would have avoided the trap, but he wasn't and after the lock was blown, Poc dove straight for the door, and through it. The grenade went off with an almighty bang, the fuel exploding an instant later. Poc was the first to burn, and the other three did not escape the destruction that ensued. The woman, passing in the street, with her dog could not avoid the blast and she went down just like the others.

In the backyard, David killed the third and then the final soldier. He had expended only six shots and killed four men. He seemed very pleased with his 'shots per kill rate', just like a training scenario, he was doing rather well. His compatriots were unarmed, and he'd kept them that way. They moved to the front of the house, to discover the damage that the grenade had wrought. No one was left standing; the old lady still writhing in pain. "Leave her!" David said as Vanny and James moved towards the body. They took no notice of his order. A sharp crack punctured the air. "Leave her, I said." He ordered them into the tuk-tuk, leaving Vanny's bike not far from the chaotic scene.

James drove and Vanny explained the directions to take and the location of the new house. Soon they were comfortable in a small, quiet villa, located just outside of town. David went straight to sleep but Vanny and James could not sleep. The poor old woman and her dog on their minds.

The following day Vanny heard the TV news, seven men had died in the gun battle. Only one man survived and he was critically injured. Poc died almost instantly, his body burning to a crisp before police investigators arrived. There was little left of Captain Poc to identify him. Again, Ken oversaw operations on the ground. Ken wondered if Roberts had anything to do with all of this, but then Roberts was on his impounded boat; Roberts had phoned Ken that very morning and asked him to visit his vessel, as it had now been searched thoroughly twice. Ken had agreed but then this mayhem had occurred and Roberts and his possible smuggling was not the priority. *Captain Poc,* Ken thought, *hadn't called in to work, perhaps he was pursuing a case?* Time would clarify the picture. In any case, Ken ordered Roberts's boat free to go. He didn't know of the missing police officer that may have made a difference, but Poc hadn't logged his concern, he had merely voiced it to achieve his video requests for surveillance.

As soon as Roberts received the release order, he moved the boat out of the dock and headed, at half speed, for the home of a friend on Fish Island; this little side trip would ensure that even if things went badly, his friends would do okay. Roberts had also seen the TV report and he had guessed that one of the dead would probably have been Poc. He seethed with anger at the death of the old woman, but he didn't know for certain that her death had anything to do with David.

When this mad circumstance was over Roberts would visit her relatives and do something for them…he wasn't sure what.

Later in the day, he phoned Vanny and David answered, "What's up old timer? What's the move?"

Roberts said, "The boat's free, let me speak to Vanny."

David responded, "No way, you deal with me now. What's the move, old man?"

"Okay, tell Vanny and James to take you to the third prescribed spot, Vanny knows where that will be."

A twisted look came across David's face. "No smart stuff, remember, I've still got your friends here."

Chapter 10
The Wheel Turns

Roberts was wearing his .38 SPECIAL snub-nose Smith and Wesson, by his side. A safety strap holding it in its leather holster. "Well, Roberts, we are armed today, hey? You know, yesterday I killed four men with machine guns, don't you?"

"I heard about that," said Roberts.

Roberts spoke with authority, "Vanny, James, make yourselves scarce, that's an order. David, you can come aboard." David stepped onto the boat, he never took his eyes off Roberts, not even for a second.

"So where's my money?" said David.

Roberts responded, "It's in the hide where we placed it. But you are not supposed to be on board. We will be underway and then you should hide, so that you are not seen." David strode about the deck, while Roberts continued to steer Menaka down the middle of the Mekong. Roberts increased speed slightly to three-quarters, Menaka's engines answered immediately, and the boat sped up. David was off balance for the briefest of seconds but controlled the change in motion.

"We can stop that now, Roberts, I'm not wanted or being chased by anyone. You know, it's only the five million that I needed to hide."

"Oh really, that's how much it is?" Roberts said.

"What you didn't count it?" Obviously, David wasn't convinced. Changing direction slightly, Roberts steered for the Mekong side of the river.

"Okay," he said, "you can be my worker. Just look useful. Maybe you can clean the deck, while we are waiting to cross into Vietnam waters?" Roberts straightened the boat and decreased the speed to half.

"What are you up to, Roberts?"

"Nothing, I figured that the Siem Reap thing was all about the money then? I just wondered how many good agents had to die for you to turn a profit?" David looked curious; was Roberts letting his guard down? Did Roberts feel something for Mary? Surely not.

He responded, "Well, does it matter, what's done is done!" Roberts was now heading down the river at a reasonable pace, the Mekong doing half the work as the boat moved with the current.

"Why did you kill Mary?"

"Are you kidding me, Roberts? She was the most dangerous fuck I've ever experienced, in my long career. I couldn't trust her, man, you know that!"

"Yeah," Roberts responded. "And the old lady?"

David screwed up his face. "Only an old lady, Roberts, you know…collateral damage. It happens in this business, all the time." Roberts had a pained look on his face.

"Not to me," he said in a low and rather personal tone. Menaka was on her own, on the river now, at least for the moment, but on this river, no one is alone for long. *It was time*, Roberts thought.

"How far are we from the border crossing?" David asked.

"It's about another day on the river and we will cross into Vietnam." Roberts vaguely pointed at David's Glock pistol, "You're not hiding anymore, but don't you think that you should put that thing away?"

David smirked, "So that you could shoot me with no consequences, don't be silly, man."

Roberts enquired, "What if I put mine away? No guns, just you and me?"

David laughed softly. "So hand to hand then, you really think that would go your way? I'm the best there is, old man!" Roberts set the autopilot, just two ropes to hold the wheel, and he lowered the speed to a quarter. Menaka jumped a little and then settled.

"This is it, David." David was still watching Roberts as an eagle watches a rabbit.

David was smirking again. "This is what?"

"We'll never reach the border, David, in a minute I'm turning around and heading home." David smiled, a sick-looking grin crossing his face for an instant.

"You'll do as I say, old man, remember, I've been watching you, anyone could drive this boat. I don't need you, Roberts."

"No," Roberts said, "I ordered Vanny to call the police at an arranged time, that time was five minutes ago, by now they'll be searching by helicopter and you'll be dead or in custody soon enough."

David smiled, "You are lying, I took their phones."

Roberts pointed to the mast where several small flags were flying. "Sailors don't need phones, and Vanny is the best there is, I trained him myself."

David was furious, his face twisted and red with rage. "I'll kill you for this, Roberts!" David stood, his face slightly towards the sun, while Roberts was under the shade of Menaka's canopy. A minute earlier, while David was preoccupied with Roberts' speed and heading changes, Roberts had removed the leather-retaining strap from his holster. David hadn't noticed. David drew the Glock from his belt, he was fast, faster than Roberts had ever been. But with the sunshine in his eyes, he wasn't as accurate as he would have hoped; Roberts had already turned his head, just slightly to the left and the bullet grazed by producing a large wound, which Roberts ignored. Roberts had already drawn his .38 and shot two to the body, without aiming…Roberts' draw was fast, faster than he imagined it could be, and relatively accurate considering he hadn't aimed his shots.

David went down to his knees, dropping the first Glock. Without a vest, Roberts' bullets had ripped through David's body. Blood poured from his wounds. One of the bullets had exited his back, causing his shirt to balloon with red. "How? How did you beat me?" David said, his strength waning. By now, David's face was flat on the deck, he could see unusual paint markings at intervals, but his life was draining out and he couldn't concentrate properly to hear Roberts' response. Holding his face, with his right hand, and with the .38 in his left, Roberts moved to stand over David. Roberts kicked the Glock to the other side of the boat, and then he tried to assist in some way.

"How did you do it, Roberts? How did you beat me?"

Roberts responded, "You were in my sweet spot. I never miss when someone is standing in my sweet spot." But David had already passed and he didn't hear Roberts' explanation.

Roberts practiced shooting once a week on his boat, in the middle of the Tonle Sap Lake. He marked out his sweet spots with paint on the deck and below, but no one knew what these strange markings were, except his brother Vanny.

A helicopter put a short burst of machinegun fire across Menaka's bow and ordered Roberts to "lay to and prepare for boarding". Roberts complied, and within ten minutes, Ken had boarded his boat with another half-dozen men. A medic saw to Roberts' face, and Ken asked some questions while drinking tea that Roberts had made for him. "What will we find, Roberts?"

"Well," Roberts responded, "that guy jumped on my boat and ordered me to smuggle him to Vietnam. He had guns, so naturally, I was doing as I was told."

Ken continued, "But you didn't do as you were told, you shot him." Both Ken and Roberts sat at a table, generally relaxed, though Roberts had begun to ache. Ken continued to sip his tea, the medic fussed with Roberts' face; there would be a large scar, the wound was deep and had just missed Roberts's carotid artery, he was a lucky man.

Chapter 11
Menaka's Back Door

Roberts was about to knock on Menaka's back door. He never went to the front door; too many people watching, and he never knew what Menaka would say or do. When he called her "Queen of Heaven" she liked it, but then, there was never a way of telling how she would react to anything or anyone. Sometimes he would say, "Menaka, Queen of Apsara, come to me." And, usually, that seemed to do the trick, but she was completely crazy, and he didn't really know how she would react to anything.

In any case, the back door flung open hitting him squarely in the face. It hurt. She didn't seem concerned at the damage done to Robert's pride or the physical pain that she may have caused him. "What are you doing here, Roberts? Get out of my back door! Stop creeping around like a silly old fool. You want something? Go get fucked!"

"I haven't said anything. Did I do something wrong?"

"You always doing something wrong, Roberts, killing people you don't know, stealing money, then giving it away. You should give to me, Roberts, not to all those other lazy shit friends of yours! Why did you not give me? Fuck off!"

Roberts was amazed at this little fireball. She would 'go off' at the slightest provocation. She couldn't be called endearing but to him she was. Like William Shakespeare's *Shrew*, she had gotten under his skin. She would never be tamed but who wanted a placid woman anyway? Certainly not Roberts. Curvy where he liked it, plump in a sexy way, and never easily understood, and it wasn't a language barrier. She was half his age, but then, she enjoyed his company, and she was never going to be an 'honest woman', her history and attitude didn't allow for that. They say everyone has a partner in this world. *And maybe,* Roberts thought, *that Menaka was his.*

Roberts sometimes thought of himself as a womaniser, stealing a girl half his age! Placing her on an evil path, robbing her of her youth!

But then, he thought, *that wasn't true.* He chased no others, he was respectful to people, especially women and children. So maybe, Roberts wasn't a womaniser, but just in love with a shrew.

Menaka was a prostitute when they'd met, and though that hadn't changed entirely she kept telling him and everyone else that 'those fucking days had ended'. Who knows, maybe she didn't fuck around anymore. In any case, Roberts wasn't giving her up.

"Baby, I've made certain that you and your family are well ahead on your house payments. Now, you are only four hundred dollars short of owning this house! You're rich!"

Menaka quietened, "So, you buy this shit hole for me?" Roberts didn't think '*yes*' should be the answer to that question, but then he was at a level of confusion that told him that no response was likely to be the correct one.

He twisted as he said it, his head nodding both yes and no, "I guess, yes?"

Her face flew into a wide smile. "You some crazy shit, Roberts!"

Her arms were flung around his neck in a hug and she landed a single kiss on his lips. "Then you better come inside and see your shitty house, Roberts, anyway, now I want to fuck you." She pulled him inside and slammed the door closed.

Epilogue
End of Conflict:
The New Beginning

"What, or who are you looking for?" Roberts said in a controlled but loud enough voice. "And what are you doing, on my boat?" The stranger swung around and stood up straight, he was about six feet tall and wore a nice suit and tie, good shoes, and a hat, which he removed to show a handsome face and slightly long blonde hair.

"I'm agent Williams, F.B.I. attached to Interpol. I'm working the 'David and Mary' case." Roberts had already decided that this guy was definitely C.I.A., but maybe not an active field agent. Roberts went along with the deception.

"I thought that case was closed. David and Mary stole five million bucks and murdered a dozen people. David murdered Mary for her share of the loot, and he was robbed by the hundred percent gang, who were chasing them for the money."

The agent pulled a face and nodded a few times. "Plausible, plausible, maybe even probable." Roberts hadn't lied and his story was pretty consistent.

Williams nodded his head again. "But why did he come back to your boat, and why did you murder him?"

Roberts wasn't much of an actor, but attempted a dramatic, slightly shocked, but indignant look, "Firstly, I didn't murder David, I have never murdered anyone." Again, Roberts wasn't lying, "And secondly, David tried to force me to take him to Vietnam. But after I had heard that he had killed Mary, his C.I.A. partner, and an old lady, with a grenade, I wasn't taking that bastard anywhere."

Williams nodded, smiling, "Good story, Roberts, is it the same story that you told your friend Ken? In any case, I don't believe you."

Again, Roberts put on his indignant face. "Which part?"

Williams looked Roberts straight in the eyes, "The part where you say, that you don't know where the money is." Before Roberts could complain, Williams changed tack, "We're not interested in the money, Roberts, you did us a big favour by killing David. We would have done it ourselves, if we'd realised what he'd done…he killed a lot of good agents."

Roberts was waiting for the catch, but when Williams stopped talking Roberts added, "Then what do you want from me? I don't have the money."

"That isn't entirely true, you banked a quarter of a million in your personal account." Roberts feigned indignance, "That was my money. Part of the deal that David made to take, well smuggle, him to Vietnam."

Williams smiled knowingly, "But you didn't, you didn't take him to Vietnam, so the money isn't really yours. But like I said, we're not interested in the money."

Williams had gotten Roberts's attention, "Then, what do you want?"

"In this country, you're an asset, Roberts. You'll work for us, and we have a job for you." Roberts had no intention of being forced to work for anyone.

"I won't do it, I'm out and I'm staying out!" He knew that a call to nationalism would be next and he was ready for it, but it never came. "Roberts, we have a job for you that our agents cannot do. It involves saving the life of a fourteen-year-old girl. You can do that, can't you? Save a life? I thought that's what Buddhists were all about. Saving people?"

END